Wa-Tonka!

Camp Cowboys

Wa-Tonka!

Camp Cowboys

Written by
Joe Novara

Illustrated by
Robert Lawson
and
Kimberly Spatrisano

PELICAN PUBLISHING COMPANY
Gretna 2006

First published by Syncopated Press, 2002
Published by arrangement with the author
  by Pelican Publishing Company, Inc., 2006

First edition, 2002
First Pelican edition, 2006

Library of Congress Cataloging-in-Publication Data
Novara, Joseph K.
Wa-Tonka, Camp Cowboys / Joe Novara.
      p. cm.
      ISBN-13: 978-1-58980-354-1
      1. Juvenile Fiction 2. Children's Stories
   I. Novara, Joseph K. II. Title.

Printed in the United States of America
Published by Pelican Publishing Company, Inc.
1000 Burmaster Street, Gretna, Louisiana 70053

Dedicated to Joe and Connie Novara, appreciators of a good story well-told and to their grandchildren whose stories are just beginning to be told: Jason, Meagan, Nikolai, Marisa, Nathan, Amy, Kelly, Dana, Lindsay, Lucia, Andrew, Michael, Paul, David, Christopher, Sean, Patrick and Anthony.

Chapter 1

Getting there is half the fun

Thoughts kept exploding like asteroids in an arcade game making it hard for Nick to fall asleep.

I wonder what the camp looks like? Will I like horseback riding? Maybe riding will be the one thing I'm good at. I never had a job before. Now I'll be a junior counselor doing dishes three times a day. But we're supposed to have plenty of free time between meals to swim and fish and play ball. At least I already know one of the JCs – Rob – sort of. Not many seniors pay attention to freshmen. Will I look weird wearing the garage-sale riding boots Mom picked up for me? My size 9 in a 13 boot? I had to cut two inches off the tops so I could bend my knees. But there won't be any girls around an all-boys camp anyway, so who cares? I've never been away from home before. I wonder if I'll get homesick?

An arm flopped across Nick's face. He shoved it away and rolled to his left. Another brother began enthusiastically sucking his thumb right next to Nick's ear to a full accompaniment of swallows, gurgles and grunts.

Naw, I'm not going to get homesick for this, he thought.

"Knock it off, Pauly!" he hissed, half-pushing, half-punching the annoying lump that suddenly disappeared from the edge of the bed. In the moment before the falling body thumped, Nick predicted the next two minutes: a moment for surprised awakening; a righteous whine: 'I'm telling'; indignant footsteps to the parents' bedroom; dad yelling; Pauly whimpering, back in bed.

The parental blast came right on cue.

"Nicky! Cool it!" his Dad hollered.

Nicky – why don't you call me Nick, like everyone else? he shouted in his head. You expect me to act like a grown up. Why don't you call me a grown up name? Nick. My name is Nick. You're always telling me, "Take over the kids while we go out for a while. You're in charge." I don't want to be in charge. That's your job. What if I do something wrong? What if something bad happens?

"Ma says to quit hasslin' me too," Pauly mewed as he crawled back into bed.

"Don't worry," Nick said, "starting tomorrow, I won't be bothering you for ten whole weeks. I can't wait to get out of here." He savored the thought of escaping to north country. Up north. It sounded so good he could almost taste it. Up north. Away from Detroit, away from this cramped house, this crowded bed.

Pauly snuffled loudly until Nick relented and laid his arm over the six year old's shoulder – gently. With that, the crying stopped and Nick resorted to an old trick that never failed to put his younger brothers and sisters to sleep: he took deep, regular breaths, as though he himself were sleeping. Soon he was sleeping as well.

The next day, Nick spent a week in the back seat of a van slowly inching its way toward Gaylord. Wedged in the jumble of suitcases and trunks, he felt marooned in a balcony watching a class reunion of the returning camp counselors.

Rob, a wide receiver on his high school football team, sat directly in front of him. Nick couldn't help admiring the arm draped along the back of the seat. The muscles stood out, hard and heavy as a marble statue's. His nutcracker jaw was shadowed by a recently shaved blue-black beard and his voice penetrated like the bass keys on a piano. Just as Nick despaired of ever looking and sounding like the model in front of him, Rob giggled. A high pitched screech like a rusty tricycle.

Well, we can't all be perfect, Nick thought with a silent sigh of relief. But he still wished his skinny arms would look something like Rob's by the time he was a senior.

"So then they called my play in the huddle, a post pattern, on third and two," Rob bragged to his captive audience.

And another thing I wish, Nick brooded while he pounded against a duffel bag to make a better pillow. I wish I could be good at some sport. I barely played Little League for one season when I was nine. Hockey costs way too much, and soccer – my Dad was always working, and we only have one car, so how could I get to soccer? And anyway, I guess I'm not much of a jock.

"Just two more miles," Jerry, the head counselor, announced as they climbed a steep hill. The circle of pink skin on his balding head peeked over the head rest every time they hit a bump in the road. 'Turtle', as the JCs called him, didn't seem to mind the reference to his padded gut and short neck.

The van chugged and lurched, slowed to a crawl, then died.

"We just got it overhauled," Turtle explained, as the car coasted to a stop on the shoulder. "Sounded like it wasn't getting gas – maybe it's the fuel filter..."

Nick crawled over bags and hopped out the back to stretch his cramped legs and look around. Pine trees. Steep, sandy hills. Something felt good. What was it? The air. The air was different. It smelled cool. Piney. Not like crowded city air. It smelled open, like he would have room to run and ride and swim.

"Who wants to hoof it to camp and tell Mack to send out the pick-up truck?" Jerry asked. Nick and Rob volunteered, starting off at a slow jog to release the day's pent-up energy. Twenty minutes later they crested a hill to find the camp spreading off to the left like a landscape for a model train. A massive, sandy hill held center place. Northern pines and chocolate colored log cabins seemed glued in a random pattern along the top and sides of the giant mound. White stones arranged in eight foot letters spelled CAMP WA–TONKA on the face of the hill.

Nick hurried over the flat land of ball diamonds and volleyball courts and slowly trudged up the steep incline to the mess hall and flag tower on the summit. He was sure that the climb would be repeated, over and over, all summer long, criss crossing like a worker ant from beach, to stable, to bunk house.

It was almost dark by the time Nick lugged his suitcase and duffel bag to the JC cabin on the far edge of the hill. The walls and ceiling reflected warm, amber colors in the light of his flashlight. Names and dates – carved with pen knives, drawn with markers, scrawled with pencil – covered the flat boards of the slanting roof. Six steel-frame bunk beds stood three to a side, heads to the opposite walls. All the beds sagged in the middle like hammocks. But he didn't mind, as long as he could sleep alone in his own private bed.

All the beds were made-up except one: top bunk, far right corner. Obviously his. He propped his flashlight on the small shelf next to the pillow and rummaged in his duffel bag for sheets and blankets. It was much cooler up north than it had been in Detroit.

Soon after Nick snuggled deep in his covers, the rest of the JC's stomped in. Cozy and excited, Nick had ring side seats as the older counselors told one camp story after another.

Rob was recognizable by his booming voice and distinctive laugh, "You guys," he began, "remember the time Otis shoved those horses into the trailer?"

"Who's Otis?" Nick asked.

"The cook," Rob replied, annoyed that his story had been interrupted.

"Anyways, these two guys – I guess they used to be campers way back when – showed up with their own horses to ride around the place for old time's sake. But when they were done, the horses didn't want get back in the trailer. So there they were in the parking lot, next to the mess hall, making a hell of a racket right when Otis was trying to take his afternoon nap."

"Where does he sleep?" Nick inquired.

"Shut up and listen," Rob snapped, "you're worse than my little brother – always asking."

"He stretches out on a bench like Snoopy on his dog house," a voice in the dark answered.

Another voice that Nick didn't recognize joined in, "And he wears this white apron that barely covers his humungous gut. And when he lays in front of the window he looks like a snow-covered mountain in

National Geographic."

"And then when he starts snoring," another unidentified voice laughed, "it's like a volcano getting ready to blow."

"Hey, who's telling this story?" Rob demanded. "So, Otis is in the middle of his nap, when all the racket starts down below. Bang! The screen door slams. We all look up. Everything stops for a second. Otis sees what's going on. He goes, 'Aargh!' and barrels down the hill, yanks one of the poles from the hitching post. Then he lines up behind the horses, grabs the pole in the middle...

"Was he pointing at them, or sideways?" Nick asked.

"Sideways – shut up, would you? – like one of those guys on a tight rope. So where was I? Oh yeah. So he charges. Man, he caught both those horses right under their butts with this pole, and then lifted them up – no lie – and shoved them into the trailer. They never knew what hit 'em. And old Otis, he just wiped his hands on his apron and went back up to finish his nap."

"That's not how you're supposed to get horses in a trailer? Is it?" Nick asked.

"Naw," someone answered, "you just lightly touch a rope across the back of their legs. You might have to criss-cross two ropes if they move their butts to one side. But it works a whole lot easier than playing Otis the weight lifter."

Easy banter circled the cabin, soothing, comforting. Nick thought, I'm going to like it here, surrounded by all these big brothers. I'll get to play little brother for a change. Someone else can be in charge.

The next morning all twelve of the junior counselors sat at one table for breakfast – the kitchen help. Two other tables were filled with college-age senior counselors. Rob elbowed the fellow next to him and winked. "Hey, Nick," he asked, "did you sleep good on your first night here?" heek, heek, heek.

"Yeah, fine," he answered, puzzled.

"Good, because that's the last good night's sleep you're going to have for a while."

"What...?" he asked, scanning his roommates. No one responded.

"C'mon, Rob, what's the deal?" Nick implored.

"You think you can just cruise into camp without paying your dues? Some night, we're going to get you." He looked around the table for confirmation. "Tonight's the night, right guys?"

Voices muttered back, "Could be." "Who knows?" "Or tomorrow." "Or next week."

"Do what you're gonna do," Nick's voice cracked. "You don't scare me."

Turtle banged a cup to get everyone's attention then tugged on the lanyard and whistle around his stubby neck. "Listen up, guys. I've got a long list here and we've got a lot to do this week before the campers get here. But before we get started, let's welcome our newest JC, Nick Finazzo."

As Nick stood up, Rob whispered, "Tonight's the night."

Chapter 2

Meeting the horses

Rob and Nick drew fence patrol as their first work-week assignment. It was their job to check the electric wire fence that circled the camp, to repair broken wire and replace rotted posts. As Nick struggled with the post-hole digger and small tools, he couldn't help being impressed by Rob striding ahead of him, a cedar log balanced on each shoulder. Muscles danced along his back and arms.

"This is an important job," Rob said without turning his head. "We have to make sure that the horses can't wander off the property if they get out at night."

"Aren't they locked in the corral or their stalls, or whatever?" Nick asked.

"Yeah. But they can always find a way to get loose at night." Rob said.

When they found their first rotted fence post, he pitched the logs forward and made a comfortable spot for himself next to a fallen tree so he could supervise Nick's digging and explain the mysteries of camp Wa-Tonka.

"The horses are coming this afternoon. They belong to old man Jaremba who rents them to us for the summer. We have to ride them every night during work-week to make sure they're gentle before the campers get here."

"Me too?" Nick asked eagerly.

"Yeah, anybody who wants to can ride."

"Is it dangerous?" Nick's voice cracked. He coughed and started again. Deeper. "I mean, I never rode a horse before. Could I get hurt? Since they're full of beans and all."

"What's the matter, you scared?"

"Nope," he said with more assurance than he felt.

"There's nothing to it, really. You can always grab onto the saddle horn if you get in trouble. It's easy to gallop. Trotting is the hardest. But you just stand up between the bumps. It's called posting. Later on, you can learn to sit the trot western style, the way cowboys do. The first rides of the season are always fun. The horses are real fresh and want to run. Later in the summer they get so worn out from five trail rides a day they get kinda sluggish."

After lunch, while Rob and Nick chalked the foul lines of the baseball field, a stake truck drove into camp. The heads of four horses swayed over the sides of what looked like a fence. Nick caught glimpses of tan, brown, and pinto between the slats. "Looks like he brought the best of the bunch in the first load," Rob remarked.

The first horse down the ramp was a buckskin with black mane, tail, and stockings. She resembled a greyhound with her slender legs, curled-under hind quarters and delicate, tapered muzzle.

"He looks fast," Nick said.

"That's Tara," Rob said "and she's a mare."

"How do you tell?" Nick asked.

"All these horses are either mares or geldings. The geldings are males that have been castrated. If they were left to be stallions, they would be too wild and dangerous around kids."

"Yeah, but," he was still confused, "how do you tell?"

"You know what male dogs look like, right? Well horses are the same, only bigger. A lot bigger. Wait till you see a gelding take a leak. It looks like half a fire hose fell out of his belly."

"Really?" Nick tried to imagine. Meanwhile, Tara galloped for a short stretch. "She's fast."

"Nah, she's okay but she's not as fast as Jamal or Prince. What she really is, is easy to ride. She has the sweetest trot. Single-foot it's called. It means you don't bounce at all when she trots. I like that. It's easier on the buns and you don't have to learn to ride Western. Tara's my favorite."

Next, a big, black-and-white gelding pounded down the ramp like a giant football player. "That's Jamal," Rob explained, "the fastest and strongest horse in the whole bunch. Period."

The next arrival was a small bay mare, almost a pony, that tugged at her halter and tattooed her tiny black hooves across the floor of the truck bed.

"Cutter is fast, but real nervous. She's always fussing with the bit and tossing her head. Not my favorite," Rob said.

The last horse was a magnificent white and reddish-brown pinto. Almost as big as Jamal but not as muscular. He pranced – ears forward, head high. He scanned right, then left, nostrils flared scoping out his new surroundings. The gelding nickered loudly, bowed his head almost to the ground and galloped out of a sharp right turn to join the others.

Nick was stunned. It was love at first sight.

"What's his name?" he asked.

"Prince. He's the next fastest after Jamal."

"That's going to be my horse this summer and I'm going to learn to ride him like he deserves," Nick vowed.

Before supper, Nick walked down to the empty stable. There were six stalls on one side, six on the other, backing on a center aisle, a large room at the far end. He ran his hand along the sapling divider to the feed trough. The wood was rough sawn, chewed into a crescent where the horse's head would go.

The tack-room door screeched on rusty hinges. While his eyes adjusted to the semi-dark interior, Nick sorted out familiar closet-smells: leather and wool, but much stronger. And new smells: sweaty blankets, burlap, dust and oats. He saw twelve saddles hanging in two rows from the wall. A bridle dangled from each pommel. A cinch strap looped the horn encircling a red, white and black striped blanket. He read the name tacked above each saddle: Jamal, Tara, Rhody, Prince, Cutter, Apache, Beauty, Scout, Shana, Jes, Rosie, and Kip. I'm looking forward to riding one of you tonight, he thought. I wish I could ride Prince. But I'll ride anything I can.

After supper, Mack, the head wrangler announced, "We got our horses today – all fat and frisky after a long winter. I need volunteers to gentle them down before the campers get here,"

Nick was the first one out of the mess hall. He ran to the junior counselors' cabin, slid into his oversized riding boots and clumped down the back side of the hill to the stable where ten other counselors were busy saddling the string.

Mack emerged from the tack room buckling his riding helmet.

"Get yourself a helmet," Mack said. "You'll ride Rhody tonight. Rob, help him with the stirrups."

Nick stepped out of the tack-room a few minutes later, helmet in place. Rob was holding the reins to a mostly white mare with a few brown patches. She looked old and tired. Nick wasn't sure what to do next. He held the back of his hand under her muzzle. It's what he did with strange dogs. The mare snuffled. Then he ran his hand along her cheek, patting.

A loud whinny pierced the air. Then a bang. Nick flinched as a stall divider speared the air from the direction of Jamal's stall.

Mack swung his lean cowboy frame onto his horse. "Well, guys," he called, "looks like we need to work the vinegar out of these plugs before they hurt someone. For the first couple of nights we'll stick to the corral – walking and trotting."

Nick scrambled into the saddle. Rob adjusted the stirrups. Rhody automatically fell in line plodding along with the rest of the horses. Nick watched the other riders, held the reins in his left hand, tried to keep his balance, not grab the saddle horn.

He was riding. Nick from Detroit was on a horse, a big horse, not like the pony he rode at a fair when he was four.

After a long slow walk that seemed to last forever, Mack called out, "Okay, let's trot a little."

Old Rhody rambled into a slow trot causing Nick to bang and bounce in the saddle. Slightly out of control, scared, Nick vowed he wasn't going to wimp out. In fact, when Mack finally shouted, "Okay, that's enough. Let's head 'em in," Nick could hardly wait to try it again next evening.

Later that night, Nick left the noisy mess hall and headed back to the junior counselors' cabin. Once past the glow of the kitchen lights he remembered how dark it was up north. No street lights and passing cars. No stars or moon. He felt as though he had stepped into a closet and closed the door. Why hadn't he brought his flashlight?

He walked slowly, feeling for steps with his feet, reaching out with his hands. He paused at a strange sound. Chewing. Then a snort. Then the thump-thump-thump of slow-moving horses' hooves. From the sound of it, the camp horses had gotten out and were grazing all around where the cabin should be. He didn't want to stumble into a horse and get kicked or trampled. What if they all stampeded in his direction?

His eyes finally adjusted to the dark and he distinguished a white, four-legged shape standing between himself and the cabin. "Rhody?" he called softly not wanting to startle the animal. "Is that you girl? How're you doing?" His voice quavered, partly from the chill night air. The horse lazily ambled over to the long sweet grass growing next to the cabin. He sprinted to the front door stoop. Safe on the tiny cement island, he suddenly felt foolish. They weren't going to hurt him after all.

The first one in the cabin, Nick found it hard to fall asleep with horses snuffling and shuffling outside his window. He missed the background noise of city traffic, sirens and distant music in the night.

After his first ride on Rhody, the rest of work-week flew by in anticipation of the evening ride. In addition to the usual job of setting the tables, serving the meals and washing the dishes three times a day, Nick helped with other camp preparations. He swept out cabins and aired mattresses, planted pine saplings on the slope behind the mess hall, strung floating ropes in the lake and painted the baseball backstop.

But every evening, no matter how tired, he was the first one down to the stables. He wanted to learn to bridle and saddle. He wanted to become familiar with each horse. But mostly, he wanted to ride. On Wednesday, after an hour in the corral, Mack took a long look at Nick and said, "I think we're ready for a short run."

At the top of the hill above the stables, someone at the head of the line yelled, "YEE-HA!!"

Rhody chugged into a slow trot. Nick bounced and jolted. As the mare picked up speed, Nick bounced even harder. Something changed. He was in a rocking chair, a big hand pushing him deep in the saddle. Another change. He was standing in the stirrups, like a jockey, floating, no longer pounding the leather. The white stones spelling CAMP WA–TONKA flew by like road signs. The JC cabin blurred on the right. He was a home run ball blasting across the baseball diamond, flying deep into center field and finally rolling to a stop at the edge of the woods.

The horses stomped and blew, danced and bobbed their heads. Nick's butt had been spanked, the insides of his knees rubbed raw. It didn't matter. He liked this place and he liked riding. In the next ten weeks he was going to spend every spare second he could find around these horses.

After supper on Friday, Mack asked Nick to saddle Beauty, a huge, round, sofa-on-legs kind of horse. She gave Nick trouble with the bridle. Whenever he got the bit near her teeth, she would lean her couch of a body against him.

Watching Nick struggle for a while, Mack finally offered some tips. "Get the bridle and bit in your right hand, Nick. Then reach under and around the horse's head. That leaves your left hand free to tickle her tongue and guide the bit into her mouth. Simple."

Sure, Nick thought, you're not standing next to the leaning tower of pizza. But he tried it anyway. Beauty easily lifted him off the ground. Hanging on with one hand, Nick used his free hand to shove a finger into the corner of the mare's mouth. The bit popped in and he pulled the bridle over her ears. It was simple, Nick thought. If you did it right.

Later as they walked the horses through cooldown, Mack rode alongside Nick and said, "You've come a long way this week. Maybe you're ready for a horse like Prince tomorrow." Nick clenched his fist and mouthed a silent YES!

The next evening, he bridled Prince and walked him out to join Mack on Jamal.

"Make sure to do the trail check: chin strap, throat latch and cinch," Mack reminded. "It's important to do that for each of the campers every time a ride goes out." His squinting black eyes warned, and don't screw up!

Nick flipped the stirrup up, ran his fingers under the strap and was surprised to find he could slide his hand under the cinch. After a second tightening, he touched the saddle with out-stretched hand and lifted the stirrup to make sure it reached his arm pit. Perfect.

"Prince is a lot of horse," Mack said. "You gotta make sure he knows you're the boss. So, talk to him in a low, firm voice. Get your reins ready, stirrup turned. You want to move smoothly. No fumbling around. Then swing up into the saddle and sit down hard. Act like you're in charge."

They started out at a fast trot that had Nick bouncing badly. He knew he looked awkward and felt worse, but he didn't care. He was riding Prince. When they broke into a slow canter, Nick could feel much more power waiting to get out.

Mack stopped at the back line of the soccer field and said, "Let's see if Jamal's still the fastest." Then he lurched forward launching Jamal into a quick lead. Prince exploded into a flat-out gallop in three strides. Nick had never felt that kind of power surging between his legs. Prince gathered himself and stretched out, the way a swimmer uncoils at the start of a race, over and over again. They couldn't pass Jamal. But for a while, just before they crossed the far end of the field, Jamal and Prince ran side by side.

On the way back to the stable Mack said, "You're doing real good. You've got enough control to ride behind the campers and make sure there aren't any problems." The head wrangler nodded to himself while appraising Nick. "Yeah. I feel comfortable with you riding shotgun on trail rides." Nick answered with a broad smile – finally a sport he could be good at.

Chapter 3

Meeting the Campers

Rob and Nick had just finished setting all of the tables for Sunday dinner. Work-week was over. The campers were coming that afternoon. The JCs walked toward the flag tower, a small square castle made of stone, the highest point in the camp. On their way up the stairs to watch for the busses, Rob teased, "You've been here a week, now. Maybe tonight's the night."

Nick wanted to say, 'Cut it out – or I'm telling.' But he stopped himself, realizing that he would sound like his younger brothers. Anyway, he asked himself, who would I 'tell'? Everyone is in on it. This is a camp tradition.

He turned to face Rob, a step below him. Their eyes were even for once. Nick might have to face initiation but he wasn't going to be bullied. "I told you before, do what you gotta do. Just skip the hype."

A number of expressions played across Rob's face in a split second: shock, unfamiliar respect and finally a predictable sneer as he sing-songed, "Tonight's the night."

They both faced the arched gateway off the highway waiting for the busses to appear. Rob broke the silence. "The busses should be here any minute now. I wonder which senior campers will be back. A couple of them have been coming here every summer for eight years and can they ever ride."

"I feel weird being a counselor to kids older than me," Nick said.

"We may be called counselors, but we're just the kitchen help. Look at it this way. Those guys pay to go to camp. We get paid to go to camp. I know I'd never get here any other way. I'll wash dishes if that's all it takes."

"Me too," Nick agreed.

A white Cadillac Seville wound it's way up the sandy hill.

"I bet that's the Vogel brothers," Rob said. "Lenny and Bruce – real pains."

Two boys, about ten and twelve respectively, shaped like fire hydrants, leaned against the car while their father lifted suitcases from the trunk.

"Look at Bruce's haircut," Rob said. "Looks like a bird's nest. Every summer their father drops them off on the first day, picks them up on the last, and they wet their beds every night in between."

Music blared over the loud speaker as the first bus pulled into the gate. Five mounted senior counselors escorted the caravan to the main parking lot.

As the returning campers poured out, Rob provided a running commentary. "There's Bobby Petzer," he whined in a mocking voice, pointing to a narrow faced, slightly stoop-shouldered senior camper wearing a cowboy hat with the brim snapped up on one side. He seemed alone in the crowd. "Looks like he's going to be wearing an Australian bush hat this summer," Rob commented. "He's the only guy who can ride Cutter bareback. Hell of a rider – but that's all he can do. You can always count on him to find a way to mess up – never gets things quite right."

"Hey, Frank!" Rob yelled and waved at a camper wearing a buttoned down, starched shirt. Frank made a gun of his thumb and forefinger, and pointed it at Rob. "Frank O'Donnell," Rob said. "Everybody's friend – great rider." Then he jumped down to help unload the bus.

Nick followed Bobby Petzer's bush hat as he separated from the crowd and headed down the hill toward the stable. If he was as good a horseman as people said he was, Nick wanted to meet him, learn from him.

"Going to see Cutter?" Nick asked as he caught up to Bobby.

Petzer's faded-blue-shirt eyes seemed out of focus, as though he had been roused from a day dream. "Huh?" he asked.

"I'm Nick Finazzo. A new junior counselor. I heard you can ride Cutter bareback."

Bobby mumbled unintelligibly, stooped to pick a wild strawberry, popped it into his mouth and continued walking.

Nick stared after the short, blond pony tail as Petzer continued down the path. I guess he just doesn't have time for lowly junior counselors, Nick thought. Well, we're both going to be here all summer. There's no rush.

A couple of minutes later, dust and sand sprang into the air as Nick scrubbed the curry comb against the grain of Prince's coat. Nick loved the powerful feel of massed muscle in the gelding's withers. His left hand followed the path down the inside of the horse's neck to his deep meaty chest. His right hand traced the curve of Prince's back as it flowed into his prominent, quarter horse rump. Absorbed in the rhythm of brushing and stroking, he was surprised by a voice, two stalls down, talking softly.

"Hey, girl. How you doing?"

He saw a bush hat partially blocked by Cutter's head.

"Ooh, that saddle sore from last summer left a big scar. We gotta make sure they get all the wrinkles out of your blanket or you're gonna be hurting again. Were you bored last winter? Huh? Did you miss me? Nobody to pay attention to you? I know how it is."

Petzer glanced up to find Nick watching. Both boys looked away, embarrassed. Nick gave two quick strokes with the brush, looked up to find Bobby staring at him. Not challenging. Simply standing tall, chin high, arms folded, implying 'here's me – what makes you so great'.

Nick held eye contact, not allowing himself to blink or look away. I like this guy, he thought. He's probably a year older than me and knows more about horses than I'll ever learn but there's something about him that says he needs help – some one to cover for him. A smile grew on Nick's face – so what if he talks to horses.

Chapter 4

Riding shotgun

Junior counselors took turns riding shotgun on camper trail rides. But on the off chance that one of the JCs was late or didn't show, Nick made sure he was around the stable grooming, bridling, saddling and generally getting in Mack's face so he would just happen to be around to fill the empty slot. He picked up a few extra turns that way.

One morning Nick got to the stable just as a senior camper ride was coming in. Bobby Petzer and Frank O'Donnell trailed the group and took a quick turn into the corral. Bobby started doing figure eights with Cutter. Frank had Tara going in the opposite direction. Nick rested his arms on the top rail, fascinated by the beauty of two horses cantering at the same speed and passing in the middle.

He listened to their chatter as they walked their horses through cool-down.

"So we were tearing through the woods between the trails – remember?" Frank asked. "I was on Kip and – who were you riding?"

"Scout, maybe, or Rosie," Bobby responded. His snake-skin cowboy boots loomed large as they passed in front of Nick who buried the scuffed toes of his garage-sale beauties in the sandy dirt. Nick thought about the seven or eight summers the two veteran campers spent learning about horses. He envied their opportunities.

Frank caught Nick looking at him, pointed his finger gun at him and nodded. Nick nodded back as he watched the next round of campers straggle down the hill for their ride. Enjoy yourself, big guy, he thought. Some of us have to work around here. I've got to ride shotgun on the next trail ride. I've got responsibilities here. Got a job to do.

A short, round camper with a bird's nest haircut lagged behind.

Nick saddled Apache, a gray pony just the right size for Bruce Vogel. As he pulled the cinch strap tight, Apache puffed up his gut. Bruce, in the meantime, leaned on the stall divider and whined, "Counselor took my Game Boy, and won't let me play with it until rest period."

"Here," Nick said, handing him the reins, "back your horse out."

Bruce grabbed the bridle roughly and Apache shied.

"Hey, pay attention," Nick scolded. "You know how to back a horse out of the stall. Now do it right."

With Apache in place, near the end of the line, Nick said, "Here, let me adjust the stirrups."

"No, I can do it," Bruce whined.

"All right, have it your way. See if I'm going to help. And put on your helmet."

The youngster fumbled with the buckles while Nick helped two other campers tighten cinches and mount up. Bruce was still struggling when Mack shouted, "Okay, guys, time to head out."

Nick unceremoniously boosted Bruce into the saddle, adjusted the stirrups, and hopped on Prince at the end of the line.

The first part of the ride was a slow walk to the lake where the horses liked to wade up to their knees and suck a long, slobbering drink. The woods came next – cool, shaded trails, perhaps three hundred yards long, one above the other along the side of a steep ravine.

Topping the ridge to the high trail, Nick caught a glimpse of Mud Lake where campers went for nature hikes. There was a cabin farther along, on the left, well-kept but unoccupied.

"Ready to trot!" Mack called. Nick enjoyed this part of the ride. The campers wiggled into their saddles anticipating a charge down the long dark trail into the bright sun of the campground – the cavalry to the rescue.

Horses accelerated, one after another, like cars at a green light. White helmets bounced up and down as the horses broke into a hard trot. Something was wrong. Bruce Vogel's head stuck out on the right. Then on the left. He was yelling. Nick let out a loud whistle to Mack as he pumped Prince. They caught up to Bruce in three strides just as the saddle rolled completely under Apache and Bruce did a slow motion tumble onto the soft sand.

Nick was checking Bruce for broken bones as Mack reined up,

"Loose saddle, eh?"

"I forgot to check it before we took off," Nick stammered over Bruce's wailing.

"Let me show you how to do it right the first time," Mack snarled as he hopped off Jamal, handed the reins to Nick, and grabbed the startled pony.

"Whoa, whoa, boy," Mack crooned gently as he removed the saddle and tangled blanket before starting over. When he pulled on the cinch strap, Apache sucked air, enlarging his girth as he had done with Nick. Mack jerked his knee, hard, into the pony's gut. The horse wheezed. Mack yanked on the strap, looped the knot, turned his black eyes on Nick and snapped, "Got it?"

"Yes," Nick answered meekly.

He gave Bruce a lift into the saddle. He could smell pee.

Riding Shotgun

Chapter 5

Are we having fun yet?

That evening, Nick wanted to be alone. He borrowed a fishing rod and headed down to the lake where he waded silently and slowly to the back end of a camp boat nosing the shore. He laid his left hand on the stern, shoved sideways, and snatched up a crayfish scrabbling for cover. He rowed a short distance to the right where a neighboring dock hung out over a drop off. He cast the bait and stretched out along the seat to wait for a hungry bass.

It's been a bad day, he brooded. A kid got hurt. My fault. Just like home. Is this fun, or what?

Footsteps sounded on the dock behind him.

"Hi! Any luck?"

It was a girl, perhaps fifteen years old, hefty but not fat. Her one-piece, emerald green bathing suit set off caramel-colored skin.

"Uhm, did you want to swim?" Nick stammered. "I'm in your way –"

"No, no," she said. "It's no big deal. I'm going to be here for two weeks. Got all kinds of time to swim. Go ahead and fish."

"Well, okay," Nick answered as he lay back across the seat. He wondered if she lived in the cabin next to the high trail.

"You with the camp?" she asked.

"Uh-huh."

"Must be a counselor."

"Junior counselor," Nick explained, "we set tables, do dishes."

"Well, that's one way to get up north. They sent me here to look after my grampa."

"Is that his place up in the woods?"

"Uh-huh."

"I didn't think anybody lived there."

"Well, he doesn't get around much. He's old – going blind. So, I serve meals and do dishes too, just like you." She chuckled warmly.

Nick liked the way she laughed. It made him feel he had known her a long time.

"It's pretty up here – clean, not like Flint where I stay," she said. "But it can get on your nerves, too. Know what I mean?"

"That's just what I was thinking," Nick replied.

"What do you do for fun?" she asked. "I mean, besides fish, which, by the way, I haven't seen you catch any yet."

"Well, I'm not the one who's talking and scaring the fish away, am I?" he teased back. "Anyway, I do more riding than fishing."

"Oh – you know what? I just realized. You all ride Jaremba's horses, don't you?"

"Uh-huh," Nick replied.

"Him and my grandaddy are buddies." The girl sat on the dock, her feet dangling in the water. "So, what do you do besides ride horses? You can't ride at night, right?"

"I don't know. I haven't been here that long," Nick

replied. "We do stuff – hang out at the counselor's cabin. Once we went into town for a burger."

"Be still, my heart," the girl mocked.

"Well, we have days off," Nick added, defensively. "Like, tomorrow's my day off, see? I get to hang out with some of the senior counselors, Jerry, Mack, Dayton – he's in charge of the beach – and this guy from my school, Rob. We all pitch in on gas and take off to water ski, or swim, or play golf. Later we go out to eat and maybe catch a movie – whatever."

"Well, that sounds better."

"Yeah, well, the best part is – I don't have to think about any of it. The older guys take care of it all. They know where to go. What to do. I'm just along for the ride."

"That's cool. Well, I think I'm ready for my swim now, if you don't mind," the girl said as she poised to dive into the lake.

Onshore, he called to the swimmer, "Nice meeting you. Catch you around."

She waved back.

The next morning, the Wednesday 'day-off' crew went to Charlevoix for a day on the beach at Lake Michigan. Nick had never swum in the big lake before, unless swimming in the Detroit River counts as part of the Great Lakes. He found it hard to compare the muddy-gray, leg-clutching current of the river to the blue-green coolness of Lake Michigan where he could see his feet on the sandy bottom in neck deep water.

The scorching day kept Nick in the water all morning. When he finally came out for lunch, Turtle was on his back reading a magazine. Mack was face down, dozing. And Dayton looked like an Olympic swimmer with his broad shoulders and long muscled arms draped around his knees. It was strange to see him on a beach without his lifeguard hat and whistle. As Nick toweled off, Jerry teased, "I see you've been riding a lot. There's no hair on your calves. You getting calluses in all the right places?" he asked. "Hey Mack, is he a hard-assed dude yet?"

"He's getting there," Mack allowed, without lifting his head.

Nick smiled to himself. It was nice to be noticed.

He must have been more tired than he realized because he slept for over an hour. He had worn a T-shirt, but forgot to cover the back of his legs. By evening he was in so much pain, he could hardly sit through supper. And when everyone got excited about driving thirty-five miles to Mancelona for a movie, he almost cried. All he wanted to do was lather up with sunburn lotion and lie on his belly forever.

Because the 'day-off' crew got to town a half hour early, they strolled around to kill time. "Hey, look," Rob yelled, as he bent over a sign in a barber shop window. "There's going to be a horse show at the Fair grounds in Gaylord. Speed 'n Action events," he read. "Key Hole, Down-and-Back, Flag Race, Pick-up Race. Sounds great. What do you think, Mack? Why don't you enter Jamal?"

"Forget it," Mack replied. "That's out of our league. Those guys start with high-class stock. And you can bet they don't let five different kids ride their mounts five hours a day all summer long. Our horses may be fun to ride," he said with a smirk, "but let's face it, they're just camp horses."

Nick was shocked. How could he say that? "Prince is as fast as any horse," he blurted out.

Mack aimed his black, gun-barrel eyes at him. He didn't like to be contradicted. "Maybe you should learn to ride before you decide how good Prince is."

Nick looked out of the corner of his eyes as he thought to himself, that's exactly what I intend to do mister. I'm going to learn to ride this summer, if for no other reason than to prove you wrong.

As they walked toward the theatre, Jerry remarked, "Maybe we could hold an event like that. A simpler version to let some of the better riders show off. Senior campers doing a horse show. I like that. Could be a good campfire night program. It's got to be better than the same old thing we always do – sit around a fire roasting marshmallows and singing songs. We would just have to start it a little earlier, that's all."

"Maybe we could even have awards, like we do for swimming. You know, best all around, most improved – like that," Dayton added.

"I know, I know," Rob jumped in, "we could give the demolition derby award to Bobby Petzer. "Or, or," he was on a roll now. Heek, heek, heek, he squeaked. "We could give Bruce Vogel the award for best trick rider."

Everyone laughed. Nick's cheeks were burning; his legs were on fire. It was a relief to hide in the air-conditioned darkness of the small-town cinema. The old fashioned seats had prickly upholstery that tortured his tender thighs. He tried sitting on his hands while Mack explained, "This theatre specializes in classic movies. When I saw they were playing **Big Country**, I knew we had to come see it. I swear the opening is going to knock you out. There is some of the best stunt riding I've ever seen. It would be worth coming all the way here just for the first five minutes of the movie."

He was right. Nick forgot all about his pain. He saw himself riding Prince at a full gallop, dropping out of the saddle, hanging on by the saddle horn, flipping over to the other side and then hopping back into the saddle. As soon as he removed his hands from under his thighs, his dreams, if not the movie, ended. He wasn't going to be riding, let alone trick riding, in the next day or two.

Are we having fun yet?

Chapter 6

Heimlich
manuever
on a snake

During the next two weeks, every time his trail ride passed the cabin in the woods, Nick looked for the girl he had met on the dock. She never seemed to be around. Clothes were drying on the line and a lounge chair relaxed in the sun. But where was the girl?

Finally, one afternoon, he spotted her at the fence, smiling at the passing line of jogging horses and bouncing nine-year-olds.

Nick pulled up for a second. "Hi! How're you doing?" he asked.

"Hey, look at you, like a bad-assed cowboy on a big mean horse," she teased.

Nick saw himself for a moment: dirty T-shirt, Detroit Tiger baseball cap, beat-up boots, sitting on Rhody. "This old nag? It's only Rhody," he scoffed.

"Don't put her down just because she's old," the girl scolded. "Besides, you'd never get me up on her. She might run away with me."

Nick flashed back to his first ride on Rhody. He had come a long way in three weeks.

Glancing down the trail at the disappearing riders, he gathered the reins; "Gotta go. I have to catch up with the ride." He hesitated a moment, patting Rhody's neck, "What's your name? I never did ask – out on the dock."

"Tanya. What's yours?"

"Nick," he answered, coaxing Rhody into a rambling trot. "When you leaving?" he called over his shoulder.

"Day after tomorrow. I might be back later in the summer."

He turned and waved.

After lunch dishes, Rob showed Nick a frog in a coffee can.

"C'mon. I'm on my way to feed the bull snake," Rob said.

Nick and Rob, like Pied Pipers, attracted a mob of curious campers as they marched to the nature cabin perched on a ledge half way down the hillside. The rickety cabin, probably a small gate house at one time, was soon jammed with boys crowding around the glass aquarium to watch Rob release the frog. In short order the snake grabbed the frog, head first, and began to slowly engulf it in its elastic mouth.

"Gross."

"How can he get his mouth all around that big frog?"

"Won't the snake choke?" Bruce Vogel wanted to know.

"Is the frog still alive?"

"How come the frog's not kicking?"

Above the sounds of their curiosity, Nick heard shouting and yelling from outside. He peered out the window to see a motorcycle rolling downhill in a collision course with the cabin. Somebody with an Australian bush hat was frantically pumping on every pedal he could reach. He wasn't going to stop.

Nick ducked. There was a loud crash. The cabin lurched. Campers stumbled back like riders on a fast-stopping bus crushing Nick against the door.

He stumbled out to find Bobby Petzer on the ground writhing, moaning, massaging his thighs with bloody hands. The motorcycle lay on its side, the fork bent, a strip of denim hanging from the throttle.

Before long, Jerry pushed through the circle of bystanders. "You okay?" he asked.

Bobby sniffed, nodded, holding back tears. "It was just sitting there – no one around – I only wanted to sit on it. I stepped on a pedal..."

"He popped it into neutral," Jerry muttered between clenched teeth.

"...and it just started to roll faster and faster," Bobby moaned. "I couldn't stop. I had to run into the cabin."

"It's a good thing," Rob said. "He would have hit the drop-off at full speed."

Jerry shook his head. "I don't think he broke anything. But he may need some stitches on his thigh. Maybe some x-rays. I'll take him to the clinic. Tell Mack to cover for me if I'm not back by supper. We'll deal with the bike later. Rob, get the camp van."

Rob complained to no one in particular, "Get Petzer off a horse and he's a walking disaster."

I guess you're right, Nick thought, as he climbed the hill to retrieve Bobby's hat. But he couldn't help feeling sorry for the camper as Jerry and Rob grabbed an arm each and half carried Petzer to the van.

Nick handed Bobby his hat through the window and received a look of gratitude from the pain twisted face.

Bruce Vogel shouted from the door of the now lopsided nature cabin, "Hey, you guys, come here! The frog got out! The frog got out!" Nick peeked in to see the first snake to lose its lunch to a Heimlich maneuver.

Chapter 7

The Mackinac* Island Cowboy

Thursday was trip day. Campers and counselors took turns going to Mackinac Island. Half went one week, half the next.

Nick had never been to Mackinac Island. The night before, he lay in his bunk pumping the veterans for details. "Hey, Rob, how long does it take to get there? What's the boat ride like? Is it true that there are no cars on the island, only horses?"

"Relax," Rob said, as he stretched his wide-receiver legs off the end of his bunk and probed a fresh pimple on his cheek. "Just think of it like a day off. Once we feed the kids, we're all done. They can't hurt themselves on the island. They rent bikes, tour the fort and buy souvenirs all afternoon. And we just go up to the Grand Hotel and sit on the huge front porch. What you do, see," Rob whispered like a conspirator, "is buy a Coke and then you get to sit on the porch all afternoon and eat free peanuts.

* *Mackinac Island and Mackinac Bridge are spelled with a 'c'. Macinaw City is spelled with a 'w'. Michiganders pronounce all three as Mack-in-awe.*

They usually charge five bucks to sit out there. But if anyone asks, just say you've checked in and are waiting for your room to get cleaned."

It took two hours to drive to Mackinaw City, park the bus, feed the campers and board the two-story ferryboat. Nick wanted to run to the rail, climb to the upper deck, check out the bathrooms and spit at the rock bass swimming around the pilings. But none of the other counselors shared his enthusiasm or interests. Instead, they walked directly to the glassed-in portion of the main deck and fell asleep, chatted or read. Nick followed their lead. As soon as they reached the open water of the straits, however, the boat began to pitch and roll. Before long, Nick felt seasick. He mumbled something about fresh air, bolted outside to the front of the boat, faced the oncoming wind and immediately felt better.

Nick decided to stay out of doors, so he clambered up the stairs to explore the open upper deck. He spotted Bruce Vogel playing a Game Boy behind a ventilation stack. Nick poked him in the shoulder, "What's up?"

"This is boring," Bruce whined. "I end up coming here four times every summer. Can't we ever go anywhere else?"

Tell me about it, Nick thought as he leaned on the rail. I should be so bored.

The Mackinac Bridge dominated the horizon. It was huge. Five miles long. How could you think to build anything that large? Nick wondered. Who would have the guts to climb all the way to the top to paint the cables?

Seagulls shrieked behind the ferry, climbing, twisting and diving like acrobatic kites. Someone was feeding them from the back of the boat – a lone figure tossing pieces of bread. Bobby Petzer.

Nick was disappointed the moment they docked. It was true that there were no cars on the island and that there were horses everywhere, but they were all heavy-boned, giant-hoofed cart haulers. They weren't enormous, marvelous animals like the Belgian draft horses he had seen at the State Fair. They were simply sturdier, droopier versions of the riding horses he knew.

Jerry gathered the campers at the foot of the dock. "Okay, let's buddy up. Lift your buddy's hand just like at the beach," he yelled. Bob Petzer and Frank O'Donnell half-heartedly raised their hands. "You can go anywhere you want. You've got your spending money. Don't spend it all at once. Just be sure to get back here by 4:00 o'clock. Sharp!"

The campers scattered among the tourists, the fudge stores, the souvenir shops. The counselors strolled up the hill to the Grand Hotel.

Nick stopped in front of Burdick's Fudge to watch a cook pour a puddle of brown goo onto a marble table top, then, using a tool that looked like a paint scraper, push back the edge of the oozing mass until it looked like a fat snake waiting to be cut into one pound slices. Rob's squeaky laugh reminded Nick to catch up with the others.

"Hey, wait up!" he called, running after Rob and Mack.

They paused. Rob pointed toward a street sweeper who was busy shoveling horse droppings into a wheel barrow. "Tonight's the night."

What could they mean? Nick wondered.

The distinctive clop-clop-clop of a horse and rider coming at a fast trot grabbed Nick's attention. The other counselors must have recognized the sound as well because they too stopped to watch. It was an amazing sight. A towering buckskin gelding with long black mane and tail, head held high, exhaled loudly with every step. Black tack sparkled with silver trim. The Martingale that restrained his head snapped as he pranced.

But more than the horse, more than the black leather, more than a real lariat looped on the saddle horn, was the rider. Nick's eyes went right to his butt. He didn't bounce. He didn't flop around. He was glued to the saddle. His body looked as if it had grown right out of the horse's back – and belonged there. He sat straight as a stick. In control. He leaned back just the slightest bit and the horse dropped down to a slow trot. He touched with his right toe and the horse cut to the right around a slow-moving carriage. No kicking. No yanking on the reins. He was driving a Mercedes by remote control.

It was as though a camera had flashed in his face. Nick was going to see this image for a long time. That's what he wanted to be. That's how he wanted to ride. That's how Prince and he were going to be.

"What a seat he had," Rob remarked as he, Mack and Nick took their Cokes and a handful of peanuts onto the world's largest porch.

"He never bounced an inch," Nick added.

"That's just what I said," Rob responded.

Well, excuse me, Mr. Horse and Saddle centerfold, Nick thought as he slouched into an enormous white wicker chair. This porch was at least as long as a football field. Jerry was already seated at the twenty-yard line with his feet up on the railing looking over the vast lawn and on to the Straits of Mackinac. Nick didn't feel comfortable about putting his feet on the railing. He felt guilty enough eating free peanuts.

An elderly woman spoke from inside the doorway, "Well, it's so nice to see you, Frank. Are your mother and father here as well?"

"No, Mrs. Cassidy. Just me, I'm afraid. I'm only here for the afternoon. Part of a day trip with camp Wa-Tonka."

Nick recognized Frank O'Donnell's voice.

"Too bad you can't stay for dinner. Listen I was just going down to Main street for some stationery. Why don't you come along. You can tell me how your family is doing."

Nick slumped deeper into his chair, hiding, as Frank escorted the woman down the carpeted front steps. A footman with a wig helped them into the hotel carriage and then snapped his whip smartly to jolt the horses into action. The loud crack of the whip got Nick moving as well. He decided to tour the island rather than watch it pass by.

First he bought a slice of fudge, then a postcard of the Grand Hotel and a ticket to the historic fort. Later, at a quiet spot on the stony beach, he sat down to write his family. On the front of the postcard, he drew a circle in the middle of the porch and wrote, 'I was here'. On the back, he started to write, 'Wish you were here,' but realized that wasn't true. Even if, by some strange chance, his family visited the island, Nick would be cast in his familiar babysitter role; shepherding brothers and sisters from ice cream stores to bathrooms to souvenir shops.

Instead, he bit into some fudge and wrote, 'Having a great time. Having fun on my own. Miss you.'

He still had an hour to kill. A faded red stable peeked out behind the Iroquois Hotel. No one was around, so Nick explored. The stalls were high-sided boxes facing each other across a narrow passage way. Nick walked down the aisle pretending to be a stable boy pouring oats into each feed trough. The local horses, just like Wa-Tonka's, had gnawed crescent moons out of the front of each feeder.

The head of an old gray nag suddenly appeared in front of him.

"Yaah!" Nick screamed.

She was the only horse in the stable. Her eyes were half closed, ears drooping.

"Why the long face, babe?" he joked. "Don't you get it?" he teased.

It was only 3:15, so he wandered back to the beach and skipped rocks on Lake Huron to kill time. About 4:00 o'clock he drifted back to the dock. Jerry called roll. No Bobby Petzer. "Frank O'Donnell," Jerry hollered, "you were buddied up with Petzer for the afternoon. Where's your buddy?"

"Sorry," Frank muttered, "we got separated."

"I'll deal with you later," he warned Frank. "All right counselors, we've got 10 minutes before the last boat leaves. Fan out. But be sure to get back by 4:15. If we can't find him, you guys go on, I'll have to stay here till he shows up."

Nick hung back for a moment watching counselors jog down Main street to check tourist shops and restaurants. "Petzer," he muttered to himself, "why can't you take care of yourself? You're older than me. Why do I have to go looking for you like you were a little kid?"

Jerry, pacing like a concerned parent, spotted Nick. "Move it, Finazzo!" he barked.

Nick automatically punched into 'find-your-brother' mode. Where would that guy go? Nick had a hunch. He jogged to the red stable, peeked in the door and saw an Australian bush hat sticking up between the stalls. Bobby was rubbing the old mare's long bony face.

"How you doing, girl? Nobody paying attention to you? Must get lonely in here all by yourself. That's the way it is sometimes. Nobody notices. Nobody cares."

"Geez, talking to the horses again," Nick muttered to himself. "Everyone else is running around the island looking for him and he's chatting with Mrs. Ed. What's his problem?"

Nick watched for a moment longer, folded his arms on his chest and said softly, "Petzer, everyone's waiting for you."

Chapter 8

Tonight's the night — finally

Nick tried to read in bed that night but couldn't stay awake. He closed his book and a moment later people were shaking him. Flashlights glared in his face. "Nicky, Nicky, tonight's the night," voices chorused behind the lights.

Three pair of hands dragged him out of the top bunk. At least it will be over, he kept telling himself. Don't over react. Jerry and Mack are here, nobody's gonna get hurt, he tried to reassure himself.

Someone unbuttoned his shirt, pulled off his jeans, left him shivering in his briefs. From the darkness beyond the lights he heard, "Out to the initiation stump, chump," followed by a familiar, squeaky laugh.

More hands pushed him outside to a stump in back of the cabin. He kept telling himself, don't fight it, just go along with it. It'll be over with all the sooner.

Nick felt slippery hands gobbing something cold and greasy in his hair, all over his body. It had a familiar smell – from the kitchen. Was it margarine?

Close. Vegetable shortening, that's what it was. They were pouring something else on his head and it was running slowly over his face, down his back. Sweet smelling, sticky, slow moving – they were dousing him with maple syrup.

Is that all? Can I go now? he wished to himself. I'm not going to react – give them the satisfaction of seeing me angry.

"Get the pillow," someone yelled. There was the sound of cloth ripping, followed by a cloud of feathers.

"Hey, Big Bird," Mack jeered, "how would you like a bun ride?" Nick didn't answer, but soon found himself leading a parade to the empty stable. Rob handed Nick a shovel, pointed to a wheel barrow next to a pile of manure and ordered, "Load her up."

After his tenth shovel full, another voice rose above the general laughter and chatter. "Now, hop on." The counselors took turns trundling him along the trail to the lake. Nick found his patience waning. What else are they going to do to me? I'm not going to take much more of this, he thought.

"Now, roll in the sand," somebody shouted. Nick obeyed. This has got to be the last of it, he seethed.

"Welcome to camp Wa-Tonka," Jerry pronounced. The party was finally over.

"I hope you all had a good time," Nick called to the departing counselors.

"We're not done with you yet, Finazzo. Go out on the dock and jump in," Rob commanded.

"Make me," Nick replied.

Rob grabbed Nick's right arm in a hammer lock and shivvied him along the dock. Nick stopped at the edge. Rob and he were the only ones left on the beach.

"This little extra is going to cost you, hot shot," Nick hissed as he reached back with his left hand, clutched Rob's sweat shirt and jumped.

Rob's shrieks of surprise and shock made up for much of the humiliation of the evening.

"I'm going to get you, punk," Rob sputtered as he splashed to shore. Nick, layered in grease like an English Channel swimmer, didn't feel the cold while he hid in the neck deep water under the dock.

Much hot water, shampoo and hard scrubbing later, Nick got back to bed for the second time that night. Just before falling asleep, he sighed, "At least I won't have to hear, 'tonight's the night' anymore."

The next morning everyone acted as if nothing had happened. Nobody said a thing. Except for Mack. When Nick brought a second helping of pancakes to his table, Mack heckled, "You don't have any extra syrup you could spare, do you?"

"Sure thing," Nick answered cheerfully, but thought to himself, you owe me. I'm part of the team now. I've been here three weeks. I've paid my dues. I'm ready to learn to ride. And I'm not afraid to ask for what I want.

Tonight's the night – finally

Chapter 9

Learning to ride Western

After lunch clean up, Nick stood outside the mess hall and looked toward the stable. The afternoon ride was out. Mack was shoveling sand into the puddles in the horse stalls. Nick strolled down to give him a hand.

"Hey, Mack, I want to learn to ride Western," he said, thinking of Bobby Petzer, Frank O'Donnell and the cowboy on Mackinac Island.

"It's your butt, you can rub it raw if you want. You're on just about every trail ride as it is. How much more do you need?"

"Yeah, but I mean, would you teach me? Can I workout with Prince?"

Mack threw two more shovels of sand, stopped, stood the shovel on its blade, propped his chin on the top of the handle and fixed Nick with his dark black eyes.

"You're really serious about riding, aren't you? Well, let me tell you, I'm no expert but I can sit a trot, all right, and I'll show you what I know. As for riding Prince, these horses work hard doing five rides a day.

They've got to last all summer." He threw two more shovelfuls. "Okay, here's the deal. You can work Prince twice a week, after supper, when it's cooler. Say, Monday and Friday. No more than half an hour. Make sure you cool him down and rub him down. Stay in the corral. No open riding. And then a couple nights a week work on some of the other horses. They can all stand a good workout with a firm hand. They tend to get bossy when little kids ride them all day."

They both shoveled while Mack talked Western riding theory. He described good posture. "When you're in the saddle, pretend there's a string tied to the top of your head that pulls your back and shoulders into a straight line." He demonstrated how feet should rest in the stirrups, heels down. "See, your heels should act like shock absorbers." He explained that cowboys had to ride this way to keep hands free for other tasks like roping. The chalk-talk went on for twenty minutes. Then the trail ride returned. Horses filed in. Campers trooped out. Nick could hardly wait for evening.

He worked Prince that night. Or, rather, Prince worked him. They trotted and jogged, fast and slow, around to the right, around to the left. Nick bounced and slapped and banged. For variety, he tried figure eights at a trot – sometimes, to ease the pain – at a canter. He was sore. The hair on his calves twisted into tight little knots and broke off. The insides of his knees felt like they had been rug burned. His backside bled from rubbing on the cantle. They worked together for a half-hour. Then Nick walked the gelding until the sweat had dried and the horse was breathing normally.

Nick was sore at first, but by mid-summer his glutes toughened up, and his leg grip increased as he exercised each of the horses in turn. He learned to work with Prince: to keep him at a steady trot, to turn at high speed, to stop with a four-legged check.

Nick talked to him all the time, "C'mon, big boy. Nice and steady. Whoa. Trot again. Slower, slower. That's it. C'mon, Prince, were gonna show 'em you're special. You and me. That's it, nice and even."

As much as he worked out, however, Nick still couldn't sit a fast trot without bouncing. He could walk fine. Canter and gallop, no problem. But at a fast trot he continued to spank the saddle.

One evening, while Nick was weaving figure eights with Cutter, Bobby Petzer appeared at the corral. Nick was more conscious than ever of slapping leather. Finally he walked the camper's favorite horse over to see him. Bobby rubbed her nose. "Hey girl," he asked, "getting a little aerobic workout tonight?"

That's right Bobby, Nick thought as he adjusted his helmet, talk to horses, not to people.

"I'm the one getting worked out," Nick said, "I can't seem to sit the trot, no matter how hard I try."

Petzer continued stroking Cutter. "Turn your toes in. Sit straighter," he offered, without looking up.

Nick nudged Cutter into a fast trot, sat tall, angled his toes inward and experienced an immediate improvement. He was starting to feel like the Mackinac Island cowboy. He was finally getting it. He wanted to thank Bobby, but he was gone, wending his way up the hill.

Chapter 10

The frog that got away

When Jerry proposed a horse show for campfire night, Frank O'Donnell and Bobby Petzer responded with enthusiasm. They joined Nick in the corral every evening for two weeks. Frank rode Tara. Bobby practiced with Cutter. The senior campers worked on barrel riding, figure eights, and cloverleafs. Nick worked with them: learning, practicing, improving.

The night before the campfire, Jerry called a meeting in the counselor cabin. "I want campers at the fire circle earlier than usual, say 7:30, that'll give us an hour before dark for the riding demonstration. Dayton had a good suggestion. We're going to give out special awards for most improved, and such, like he does for the swimming program. If you have someone who could use a little recognition, let me know. We'll fit it in. I want Rob and Nick to get the firewood."

The next evening, Rob and Nick hauled deadfalls out of the woods. "Yuck!" Rob complained as he dropped his load in a heap near the center of the fire circle. "Dirty job. Mosquitoes." He waved his hands around his head to drive off the bugs that had followed him out of the woods. "I hate it. Why did he pick me?"

"Where're you going?" Nick asked, as Rob started up the hill.

"I'm going to get some insect repellent before I get eaten alive."

Nick was prepared for this problem and had a small squeeze bottle of OFF in his back pocket. "Hold on," he shouted, "I've got some right here." He didn't add that he was sure Rob wouldn't come back and that he would be left to finish the job alone.

"Give it here," Rob demanded.

Nick was helping Mack set out barrels for the cloverleaf when Jerry's voice blared over the loud-speakers, "Campfire starts in 15 minutes. We've got a special surprise tonight. So hurry down and get good seats."

"This should be fun," Nick said.

"Yeah, I guess. Shows the younger kids what they can learn to do over the years."

"Mack, how do you rate Frank and Bobby as riders?" Nick asked.

"Frank has learned a lot. But Bobby can teach him things. That Petzer kid has a natural seat. And he's got a touch with horses – what a gift."

"But he's always messing up," Nick objected.

"Not like some folks we know," Mack replied. Before Nick could defend himself, Mack added, "Besides, we can't all be great at everything. He's young. He'll learn."

The campers sat on logs forming a giant U in front of the unlit campfire as Frank and Bobby trotted their mounts onto the meadow beyond. Nick sat among the campers to better survey their reactions.

"That's Tara. I rode her yesterday."

"I want to do that some day."

"How come Cutter never does that for me?"

"That's neat, look how she swoops around the barrel!"

Everyone applauded as Frank and Bobby walked the horses through cool-down. Nick began to worry when Jerry got up to announce riding award winners. He wasn't going to embarrass me by giving Bruce Vogel an award, was he? Nick wondered.

"And for the ten-and-under, most courageous rider award."

Nick hunched his shoulders and grit his teeth.

"Bruce Vogel! Bruce where are you? Stand up and come get your award."

Everyone looked around. No Bruce. Dayton, his cabin counselor, stood up, "He came down here with us. Where could he have gone?"

Jerry turned to Frank O'Donnell, "Before we get all worked up here, Frank, why don't you ride up to the johns, see if he's there. Then check his cabin."

Frank swung onto Tara and rode up the hill.

"And now for the most improved rider..."

A few minutes later, Frank reined in next to Jerry and shook his head – no.

Turtle puffed out his cheeks, crossed his arms and tilted his head sideways in thought. No one spoke. He beckoned the counselors to one side. "It's getting dark fast and we have to move quickly. Mack, I want you to organize a search party. I'll continue here with the campfire. The rest of you counselors meet with Mack by the stable." Then he turned to the campers and boomed in a cheery voice, "Okay, who wants to light the campfire? Anybody?" Kids whined and pleaded and waved their hands while the counselors, along with Frank and Bobby on their horses, followed the head wrangler to the stable.

"Bobby. Frank." Mack barked. "Take your horses, while there's still some light and ride the trails. Frank take the bottom trail. Circle by the beach just in case he wandered down there. Bobby take the upper trails. Rob go get as many flashlights as you can. Rally point will be the high trail at the edge of the woods. The rest of you fan out through the woods. Give yourselves ten minutes, then get a flash light from the rally point."

Nick slid into the shadows behind a tree. "Why are people always telling me to look for lost kids? I came here to get away from all that," he grumbled to himself. His thoughts were interrupted by Lenny Vogel, Bruce's older brother, tapping him on the arm.

"I want to help look for Bruce," he whined. Nick shuddered. I hate that whine, he thought. Reminds me of fingernails scratching a blackboard. And something else – he sounds just like my brother, Pauly.

When Nick didn't answer right away, Lenny pleaded his case. "He might be hurt and I want to, you know, help, if I can."

Nick studied the outline of the young camper in the gathering darkness – looks like a forty gallon shop vac, he mused – worried about his little brother. Like I would be for mine.

"Huh, can I?"

Nick shook his head. If I wanted to get away from kids, I guess I shouldn't have come to a summer camp, he thought.

Nick hunkered down. "This is a job for the counselors," he said. "But if you really want to help, try to think of where your brother could have gone."

"He hasn't been too excited about horses lately." Nick frowned at the reminder. "Maybe when he saw the horse show, he just took off." He paused, then added, "He's been all excited about frogs the last couple of weeks, ever since he saw the bull snake eat one in the nature cabin."

"Where does he go to catch frogs?"

"Mud lake, mostly."

"Thanks, that's a big help," Nick said. He patted Lenny on the shoulder as he tried to picture the path to Mud lake – down a ravine from the high trail.

The woods were so dark, Nick could barely see. He had to look up to the lighter sky and follow the opening between the tree tops to stay on the trail. "Bruce. Hey, Bruce," he called from time to time. He could see the last of the light reflecting off the water. He was almost there.

"Here, I'm down here," a high pitched voice answered.

Good, at least I found the little brat, Nick sighed. The mucky dampness of the water's edge rose to meet him as he felt his way down the path. "Bruce, where are you?" he called.

"Here, by the water," the small voice mewed.

Nick waded into the soft goo, sliding one hand along a fallen tree branch. The muck came up to his knees before he could feel bottom. Then he saw him: Bruce was tangled in the branches.

"I'm stuck," he cried. "I was trying to catch a frog. Then I slipped. And my leg hurts and I can't get out."

Nick grabbed him under the arm pits and lifted gently. "Ow, my leg." The camper started to cry. Nick ran his hand down Vogel's leg to the ankle. It was wedged between tangled branches. Nick grabbed the main branch with both hands and heaved. Bruce's foot popped free and Nick was able to lift him out. His added weight, unfortunately, made it even more difficult to walk ashore.

On the beach, Nick asked, "Can you walk?"

Bruce stood up, yowled, and plopped back down. "No, it hurts," he wailed.

"Shhh, I think I hear something."

"Bruuuce, Hey, Bruce!"

"Down here, we're down here." It sounded like Bobby Petzer. "Is that you Bob?"

"Yeah."

"Listen, Bob," Nick thought fast. "We need flashlights to get out of here. So go get some from the rally point. Then see if you can get Cutter down here so we can carry Bruce out. He's too heavy for me."

"Is he hurt?"

"Maybe a broken ankle, probably just a bad sprain."

"I'll be right back."

They heard a thump on a horse's ribs and the sound of a fast trot heading out of the woods.

Bruce started whining, "My ankle hurts, and my mosquito bites itch."

"We'll get you out in just a bit," Nick reassured the frightened youngster while he reached in his back pocket for insect repellent. "Well, at least we can keep you from getting bit from now on. Let me put of some of this bug juice on you."

Before long they heard hoof beats approaching.

"Bob – down here," Nick shouted.

Petzer lit the trail with a flashlight and soon he and Cutter were standing on the shore. Petzer aimed the light at Bruce's ankle and asked, "How's it look?" Nick tried to wipe off the muck but stopped when Bruce cried and squirmed from the pain.

"Let's immobilize it," Nick said. "Then you can carry him out on Cutter." Bob's flashlight found a dead tree with peeling bark. While he broke off two pieces, Nick slipped his belt off. They snugged the bark around

Bruce's ankle and secured it with the belt. Once Bob was in the saddle, Nick hefted Bruce up to him.

"You better walk ahead with the flashlight," Bob suggested, "I've got my arms full."

Moments before the strange procession reached the ridge trail, headlights illuminated the path. Mack drove up to meet them.

The senior counselor reached for the injured camper and in a voice soft with concern asked, "How're you doing, Bruce?" That's when Bruce lost it. Between his sobs, Nick explained about the ankle.

"We'll have you looked at in a jiffy, little guy. You two," Mack said to Bob and Nick, "can get cleaned up. We'll take care of it from here. Oh, and thanks. You did good – both of you."

Bob took his left foot out of the stirrup and said, "Hop up." Nick swung up behind him.

As they wound their way past the abandoned campfire, Petzer spoke. "You started calling me Bob tonight, instead of Bobby. I like that."

"It fits," Nick replied.

Chapter 11

Trotting up to the Drive-in

The next morning Nick went to see Bruce in the infirmary. From the doorway, he could study the camper propped in a hospital bed; his ankle elevated and ballooned to basketball proportions with Ace bandages and ice packs.

Poor kid's gonna miss a lot of activities in the last two weeks of the season, Nick thought. He felt so heavy last night, but this morning he looks like a baby bird, all alone in a big white nest. A familiar smell of ammonia reached Nick – the bird had wet the nest.

"How's it going, Gimper?" Nick asked.

"Okay," Bruce whimpered in a self pitying, 'be careful, I hurt myself and am very fragile at the moment', voice.

"So tell me about that frog. Was he worth it?"

"Oh, man, he was huge." Bruce sat up in bed, a different person. "I kept thinking, that bull snake will never be able to swallow him. And I had him. Man, I had him. That's when I slipped."

Mack leaned in the door, "We're going into town to get that ankle x-rayed. Ready, Bruce?"

"Not yet," the nurse said, carrying an armful of fresh bed linens and clothes for Bruce.

"Hey, Finazzo," Mack said as they waited outside the cabin, "see what you think of this. Jerry wanted to do something special for you, Frank and Bobby. I suggested a horseback ride into town. How does that sound?"

"Great! And if we could get him to spring for a burger and shake, we could ride into the drive-in and order from horseback."

"I'm sure that can be arranged."

Early the next evening, Mack, Bob Petzer, Frank O'Donnell and Nick mounted up and trotted toward town and the Toot'n Tell Drive-in. Prince pranced and flared his nostrils as though he knew this was a special occasion. Tara and Cutter were excited as well. "Come on, Mack, let's see if Jamal can still take us all," Nick challenged.

"Nope. Not next to the highway. It's too dangerous. Besides we've got a six mile round trip ahead of us. A nice steady trot will do just fine."

They passed the place where the van had broken down, where Nick took his first breath of north country air. It seemed so long ago – longer than seven weeks. He had learned so much. Who would have thought he would be riding into town in control of a magnificent horse, holding his own with experienced riders?

For all his fast learning, Nick couldn't be part of the history, the many summers, that Mack shared with the campers. All the way into town, the new JC felt left out as the others recalled past overnight horse trips. He gathered that Otis would pack groceries for supper and breakfast. Then the food, sleeping bags, and other gear would be dropped off at a prearranged campsite.

"Remember that time, Mack," Frank asked, "when you told Bobby to dig the latrine at our campsite?"

"Hey, come on, it was all rocky there. I couldn't dig two inches without hitting boulders," Bob said.

"So you stacked up sharp, jagged rocks into a kind of toilet bowl."

"Gimme a break, that was two summers ago. Besides, it didn't seem like a bad idea at the time," Bob responded. "At least I didn't burn a hole in the foot of my sleeping bag from sleeping too close to the fire."

"It was cold that night," Frank explained.

"And scary – especially after we heard all those strange noises in the bushes," Mack teased. "Seems to me, some folks hogged more than their share of the fire."

"Hah, those noises probably came from someone trying to find Petzer's sorry latrine. But, hey, we were pretty cool last night, huh, Mack?" Frank bragged as he leaned in and out of the saddle pretending he was barrel riding in front of the campers.

"You looked good," Mack said.

"We not only looked good, we were good," Bob laughed, "I bet Tara and Cutter could beat any horse around these parts."

Nick finally had something to contribute. "Mack doesn't think so. Mack thinks our horses are nags."

There was dead silence as Frank and Bob slowly turned to stare at Mack. They looked like two kids who had just been told there was no Santa Claus.

"C'mon, Nick," Mack hedged, "I never said it like that..."

Bob interrupted, "Now, wait a minute, Mack. We're not talking about Rhody and Beauty and Apache. They're camp horses. Okay? We're talking about these four horses, the best in the stable. You honestly don't think Cutter or Prince couldn't stand up to real competition?"

"And what about Tara?" Frank added.

"Look, all I'm saying is, you can't expect horses, I don't care how good they are, that are ridden by thirty different campers a week to compete with a horse that's been ridden and trained by one rider."

"What about last night then," Frank asked, "was that just a nice show? A piano recital? Is that what you're saying?"

"No," Mack responded. "Last night was fine. You guys are good riders. You just have to know your limits, is all."

The campers were quiet, pondering Mack's words to the steady tattoo of trotting hooves. Finally Bob turned in the saddle, his faded blue eyes suddenly arctic ice. "You're wrong. You know that, Mack? Flat wrong."

My sentiments exactly, Nick thought.

A while later, Nick broke the silence. "Mack," he asked, "is there a chance I could go on the overnight with you guys next week? It's the final ride of the summer."

"It's the final ride, period," Frank said. "I won't be coming back next year."

"Me neither," said Bob. "I'm getting too old."

"We ought to do something special on this last ride," Frank said to Bob. "You know – something to remember us by. The kind of thing they'll talk about around the campfire when we're gone."

"Like what?" Bob asked.

"I don't know," Frank continued, "but when we see it, we'll know."

Ignoring their chatter, Mack responded, "I don't see why you can't come with us, Nick. I'll check with Jerry."

At a stop sign near the edge of town, Mack snapped Jamal to a halt and called out in a coach's voice, "Listen up, guys." The younger riders swung their horses around to face him. "I want you to ride single file. Keep your horses on tight rein. They can get spooked by loud noises. And no show-off, funny-stuff, Okay?"

People stopped to stare and point as the horses trotted down Main street. While they waited for a light to change, a lady in the next lane rolled down her window and asked, "Where y'all from?"

"Texas," Mack drawled. "Been riding since May."

"Well, we're from Dallas ourselves. We've come to see our daughter in Petoskey." The light changed. As the car pulled away the woman called out the window, "You boys have a good time now, hear?"

They laughed all the way to the drive-in where they each pulled up to a speaker phone and menu box.

"May I help you?" the box squawked in Prince's ear. He jumped and snorted, banged into Jamal.

"Easy, big boy." Nick tried to calm Prince down. "Whoa there. Easy, big boy".

"Big Boys? We don't serve Big Boys – just regular hamburgers, shakes and fries."

"Fine," Nick shouted to the box as Prince fussed and sidestepped. "I want a hamburger, strawberry shake and fries."

"Just a minute," the box said.

A pretty brunette waitress came out to take the rest of the orders. When she got to Frank, she stopped to let Tara nuzzle her hand. "What a nice horse. What's his name?"

"Her name is Tara," Frank said. "What's yours?"

"Kim," she smiled sweetly, still stroking the horse's muzzle. Tara snorted. "Yuck, horse boogers," the girl wailed as she held her arm out from her body, wrist dangling. She scowled at Frank. "How rude!"

"Maybe we should just dismount and eat at the picnic table in back," Mack suggested.

Chapter 12

Staying alive at Deadman's Hill

Six campers stood in the morning sun listening to Mack lay out the trip. Frank massaged Tara's nose. Bob patted Cutter's shoulder. Nick was assigned to the horseback campout. The last overnight of the summer. The last trip ever for Frank O'Donnell and Bob Petzer.

"It's a ten mile trip to our campsite in Jordan Valley," Mack said. "We'll stop at Deadman's Hill for a break. We should make camp around 5:00 o'clock. Here are some rules I want you to follow. Don't go near the highway if you can help it. Stay behind me and follow my signals. We'll trot and run a little. But plan on doing some fun riding when we get to the campsite. It's all quiet dirt roads back there. All set? Let's head out."

Nick rode shotgun as usual; but found the new scenery more interesting than the well-known Wa-Tonka woods. About a mile down the road, the group passed Jaremba's General Store. There was a huge meadow in back and an old barn. "Recognize your winter home?" Nick asked Prince who seemed to neither notice nor care.

There was an historical marker in the parking lot for Deadman's Hill. The name, it seemed, came from an unfortunate lumberjack who was crushed by a logging cart that broke loose on the steep bluff. What steep bluff? Nick wondered. He had seen nothing but flat land for the last few miles. He dismounted to stretch his legs and followed the arrows up a slight rise, where, like an airplane flying over the edge of a mountain, the ground dropped out in front of him. At his feet lay a twelve mile long valley with a stream twisting along its floor. Jordan Valley. It was like a giant scratch on the earth's surface.

"Off there on the left, where the bluff meets the valley floor, is where our camp will be," Mack informed the campers. "We've got three more hours of riding, guys."

"Hey, Mack, is it true that some of our guys took a canoe down this bluff and paddled that river down there?" Frank inquired.

"A couple years ago some junior counselors tried that. They got down. But the river is more like a stream – clogged with dead falls and brush. We had to come in on the road and haul them out."

Mack led four of the campers along the access road. Frank, Bob and Nick trailed behind. Frank asked in a deliberately casual way, "You guys ever see the movie, Man from **Snowy River**, where these Australian cowboys go barreling down the mountainside snapping their whips, chasing a herd of wild horses?"

"Great movie," Bob replied.

"I was thinking of that bluff back there." Frank paused, "If you can get a canoe down, I bet we could get horses down."

"Ummm, sounds like the stuff of legends," Bob mused.

"Hey, guys," Nick said. "These aren't Australian mountain ponies. And we're talking Deadman's Hill. Besides..."

"And then," Bob interrupted, "when we get to the bottom, we can ride along the road to the camp and be roasting hot dogs when the other guys get there."

"Yeah, let's go for it," Frank shouted.

The riders had stopped. Nick stood between the two campers and the bluff. He held up his hands as if to push them back. "You can't do this. Mack wants us to stick with him."

"Go tell Daddy," Frank challenged. "By the time you get back, we'll be on our way down."

"Besides," Bob added, "what are they going to do to us? Kick us out of camp with one week left in the season?"

"Bob!" Nick yelled.

Petzer stopped.

"C'mon," the rookie counselor pleaded, "don't do this to me."

"Lighten up, Nick. This isn't about you," Petzer said. "Besides, I don't need a mother. I already have one."

Both campers chucked their horses in the ribs and galloped for the bluff.

Nick turned Prince in a circle trying to decide what to do. It really wouldn't do any good to ride ahead, to tell Mack. Probably it would be better to stick with the campers in case something went wrong. "Yaah!" Nick yelled as he launched Prince into a gallop, racing to the edge of the ridge where he heard laughter from the riders making their way down the wall of the bluff.

Nick heard them – first on the right, then on the left – but couldn't see them. The slope must have been very steep if they had to zig zag down the face of it.

"Well, we're not doing any good standing around up here, Prince," Nick said, easing the gelding over the edge into the dense brush surrounding the path. It became clear, very soon, that there was to be no return back up the slope. The bluff was so sheer that Nick was able to touch the side of the hill as they traversed. At times Prince struggled to keep from sliding sideways. Finally, Nick had to dismount and lead his horse.

He stopped. The laughing and shouting had ceased. He stepped around a bush and there were Frank and Bob on the valley floor, on foot, facing a wall of brush and tag alders.

"I didn't expect to find all this underbrush," Frank moaned.

"Well, we can't go back up and we can't go forward. The trail goes off to the left for a while. Let's follow it," Nick suggested.

Twenty yards ahead, Bob stopped and called back. "The trail ends and the ground is soft and mucky. I can see the stream. It's just twenty feet away."

"Guys," Nick called, "leave the horses for a minute, come back here and let's talk this over."

In a small clearing, just big enough for the three of them to sit down, Nick asked, "Any ideas?" The campers shook their heads. "Well, we've got to stick to the original plan," Nick remarked, "keep going forward. But how are we going to get through all the brush and muck on this side, and the other side too, before we get to the road?"

"We could probably get through," Bob offered, "but what about the horses?"

"If only we had a bush saw or an ax," Frank thought out loud. "We could clear a path for the horses."

"And then," Nick jumped in, "we could lay the brush across the mud to firm up their footing."

"Wait a minute," Frank said. "They always pack a saw and ax with the food and bed rolls. They should be sitting at the campsite right now."

"Sure," Nick said, "but how are we going to get ourselves out, get the tools here, and then get back to the campsite before Mack does?"

There was a long silence broken only by the whine of mosquitoes.

"I can do it," Bob said quietly.

"How?"

"Like this. Cutter's smaller than the other horses right? I take off her saddle to reduce weight. Then I lead her through the brush – I can coax her through. Then I ride the stream for a while till I find a good spot to get out on the other side. Then I ride to camp. Get the tools. Ride back. And if we're lucky, we still might pull the whole thing off."

Nick stuck out his hand, palm up. Bob slapped his on top. Frank laid his on Bob's.

Nick and Frank watched Bob thread Cutter through the dense underbrush. At one point, when Cutter hesitated, Bob stopped as if there was nothing else on his mind, and talked to her. "Don't be scared, girl. You know we can't stop now. We have to go forward. We can do it. One step at a time. Come on. We can do it."

Nick wondered if he was talking to himself, and to them, as well.

"I'm in the river!" Bob yelled. "Yow! It's cold. But at least the bottom is hard."

A minute later, there was a distant, "Yah!" followed by the rhythm of racing hoof beats.

Nick and Frank hunkered down on the trail for a long wait. A cloud of mosquitoes moved in. When it got to the point that they were slapping almost constantly, Nick grabbed a handful of mud, and smeared it behind his neck and along his arms. Frank turned up his nose, "How can you stand to put that glop on your skin?"

Well 'Mr. Neat and Clean', we're not riding in Grand Hotel carriages here, Nick thought. If you had gone through an initiation, maybe you might be able to handle a little glop too. Besides, it wasn't my idea to come here.

Several mosquito bites later, Frank overcame his repulsion, and gave himself a Jordan River mud bath too.

Then there was nothing to do but wait.

Finally, they heard hoof beats coming down the road. They shouted. Bob shouted back and soon his white helmet was visible through the brush.

They sawed, and chopped and cross hatched the brush making a single file trail to the river. As soon as Nick and Frank led their horses out, they whipped off their shirts and washed crusted mud from their necks and faces in the cold, clear water.

"About thirty yards downstream, there's a solid bank and the road runs right next to it." Bob's eyes were dancing. "After that we've got a hard 30 minute run to the campsite. What time is it now?"

"Almost 4:30," Frank answered with a big grin. "This is do-able, guys. Plan A is back on schedule."

The trio raced into the campsite just before 5:00 o'clock. The horses were lathered up, Cutter especially. Her ribs were heaving and she was covered with sweat – exhausted. Nick took the saddles off the horses and walked them through cool-down. Meanwhile Bob and Frank started a fire and broke out the hot dogs. Around 5:15, Mack showed up with the others.

"What took you so long?" Frank asked.

Mack gave them his game face. He wasn't pleased. "You guys find a short cut?"

"Something like that," Bob answered.

"Well, after we're done eating, I thought we would take a fun-run back down the road till we're about opposite the bluff. How's that sound guys?"

Frank and Nick nodded, "Sure, why not?"

"Not Cutter," Bob said softly, "she's played out."

"I see," Mack replied. "Actually I wasn't inviting you three. I want Nick and Frank and Bob to finish setting up camp for the rest of us. Cut enough firewood for tonight and tomorrow morning. Rope off a corral. Lay out ferns for bedding. Dig a latrine." Then he rode off with the remaining campers.

Nick, Bob and Frank watched the riders round a bend in the road, then turned and gave each other high fives.

Chapter 13

One last — something

Tired as he was, Nick found it hard to sleep. First the ground was too hard. Then all of his mosquito bites began to itch at once. Evening mist slowly invaded his sleeping bag like a cold, penetrating rain. And when he finally began to doze off, visions of steep cliffs, dense bushes and swarming mosquitoes startled him awake. It was a long night.

Nick woke to a soggy sleeping bag drenched in morning dew. He staggered around slumbering campers strewn about like piles of wet laundry to join Mack by the smoking fire.

"Can I help with anything?" Nick asked.

Mack responded with an accusing glare. Nick quietly withdrew to tend to the horses. By the time he had brushed and grained each of them, the sun was burning off the morning mist, campers were rolling up sleeping bags and Mack was serving scrambled eggs and Otis cinnamon rolls.

On the return trip, Frank, Bob and Nick rode together behind everyone else. There wasn't much to say. Not after all the excitement of the day before.

When they passed Jaremba's, they knew they were getting close. They couldn't let the summer end like this. They all felt the need for one last – something.

They stopped their horses in a line. A starting line. A ribbon of grass stretched in front of them, running between the highway on the left and the camp on the right. It was perhaps two football fields long and about as wide as a two lane road. "First one through the gate," Bob yelled, as Cutter shot forward on the outside. Prince was after her in a flash. Frank and Tara were soon far behind. Prince caught up in no time and stride by stride, pulled past Cutter. Nick half turned in the saddle and shrugged at Bob, as if to say what can you do when you've got a horse like this? Then Prince started veering to the left, toward the highway. Nick yanked on the reins. Fought to bring him back to the right. Prince kept leaning and angling left. Nick tugged with all his might. Prince finally straightened out. That's when Nick saw the ditch. The ditch across the beautiful race track. The ditch Prince was wisely trying to avoid. And that was when Prince decided to jump. Nick almost flew from the saddle. One foot came out of a stirrup. He managed to lurch against the saddle horn and grab Prince around the neck as they soared across the six foot gap. What a jump!

A diesel horn blared. A horse screamed. Nick turned to see Cutter thrown in the air by a semi. Nick felt his stomach sink like when an elevator stops too fast. Cutter landed on her side next to the highway.

Please, God, he prayed. Don't let her be hurt – not that beautiful horse.

The three riders reached Cutter at the same time. Her eyes were wide with pain and fear. Her legs quivered as she thrashed her head from side to side.

"I think her back's broken," Frank said.

The truck driver leaned in. "I'm sorry, guys. She ran right in front of me."

"Only because you blew your horn. That's what made her panic," Bob cried. "She shouldn't suffer like this."

"I keep a gun in my cab," the driver said.

"Get it." Bob ordered. "Fast."

When the driver brought his gun, Bob said, "Give it to me." Then without a moment's hesitation, he walked up to Cutter and shot her in the head. When she lay perfectly still, he knelt next to her and stroked her for a long time.

That afternoon everyone pitched in to dig a large hole to the right of the gate. Jaremba came by with his tractor and dragged Cutter into the grave. Bob climbed in to cover her with his parka. Then he took off his Australian bush hat and laid it on the parka. Campers and counselors took turns filling in the grave.

After the burial, Nick walked to the lake. From the far edge of the beach he watched campers raising paired hands for the last 'buddy check' before the end of afternoon swim. In a few minutes he would have the swimming area to himself.

Kick – glide. Kick – glide. Nick forced himself to swim slow, deliberate laps, trying to sort his jumbled feelings in the soothing rhythms of breast stroke, side stroke, back stroke and crawl.

"Hey, Cowboy Nick!" a female voice called.

Nick swam toward the dock. "Hi, Tanya. You made it back."

"Yeah," she answered, kicking arcs of water with her feet, "Grandpa missed me."

Nick had never been this close to her before, never noticed her eyes: hazel, long lashed, welcoming. He deliberately rested his upper arms on the decking to make his biceps appear bigger.

"How come you're swimming, cowboy, and not out there riding those mean old horses?"

Nick winced. Looked away.

Tanya pulled her feet onto the dock, wrapped her arms around her knees and began again, the teasing tone gone from her voice. "Sorry. I didn't think. Jaremba stopped by after lunch and told us about the horse that got hit by a truck."

Nick focused on the far side of the lake.

"He said some campers were racing next to the highway. Sounded like a terrible accident."

"Yeah – an accident," Nick replied tonelessly. "That's what it was – an accident."

"Jaremba said one of the kids was really broken up when they buried the horse. Was he the one riding?"

Nick nodded.

"Did he get hurt?"

"No. Just the horse."

"Were you there?"

Again Nick nodded.

"Oh," Tanya replied thoughtfully. "I see." She paused for a moment. "My girlfriend and I, once, saw my cat get run over by a car. It was gross." A convulsive shudder ran through her body.

Nick looked up, waiting for more.

"Then people tried to tell me, 'It's Okay, you can always get another cat.' I didn't want another cat. I wanted my cat and I knew there wasn't anything going to bring it back. I just had to live with that."

Nick shivered. "I'm getting cold – better go in."

As he stroked toward shore, Tanya offered, "You know, people say, if you fall off a horse, you're supposed to get right back on – but what do you do if the horse is dead?"

After supper Nick walked over to Mud Lake to sit and think for a while. Bob was there.

"She didn't want to jump," he said in a flat, toneless voice, as if he were testifying in a trial. "Maybe she saw the ditch too late – was as surprised as I was." Bob stared out over the water. "She planted all four feet at once. I flew. Then I heard the horn." He paused. Thought some more. "She was too small. Probably couldn't have made the jump even if she knew it was coming." He turned to Nick, his lips pressed together, the corners of his mouth working. "Why do I always mess up?" he asked. "How come I never seem to get anything right?"

Nick reflected for a moment, replaying recent events. "That's not true," he replied. "You helped Bruce Vogel, right here. And look at what you did in Jordan Valley. You got us out of a jam at Deadman's Hill."

The sunset reflected in Bob's eyes, but Nick was sure he wasn't watching it.

"Besides, you would never hurt Cutter on purpose," Nick added. "It was an accident –"

" – that could have been avoided."

No argument there, Nick thought. And now Cutter's gone and we can't get her back.

They sat together in silence until it was dark.

One last – something

Chapter 14

Making it up to the campers

Like mourners at a funeral parlor, the entire staff gathered in the counselor's cabin that night; subdued, seated on sagging couches, listening to Jerry. The screen door banged. The head counselor paused. Everyone turned to stare at Nick in the doorway. He was responsible for this funeral.

Jerry continued, "The kids are down. We're down. And we've got another week to go till the end of the season. We can't let it end like this. Anybody got any ideas?"

Nick felt bad about many things: what Jerry had just said about camp morale; about losing Cutter; but especially he felt like the kid who had just ruined the family vacation. Nick didn't like that feeling. He wanted to make things right. Finally, he raised his hand, cleared his throat so his voice wouldn't crack and began, "Seems like we ought to do something with horses. Like the way you're supposed to get right back in the saddle when you fall off. Right, Mack?"

The head wrangler kept his eyes down – barely nodded.

"Well, remember that horse show we saw advertised in Mancelona? I think it was scheduled for this week or next."

"It's gonna be next Thursday, at the County Fair," Rob recalled.

Dayton, elbows on his knees, twirled and caught his lifeguard hat. "What's your point, Nick?"

Nick thought fast, remembering Bruce Vogel's complaint about going to Mackinac Island all the time. "Thursday is trip day. I think we should go to the County Fair instead of Mackinac Island. Campers are getting tired of going there anyhow. And I think we should enter some of our horses in the competition. The campers can spend the day at the fair and then watch us perform in the horse show."

"You mean make fools of ourselves," Mack jeered. "I told you before, these camp horses of ours can't compete with serious show riders. I'm not going to get laughed at."

Other counselors nodded in agreement.

"I'm not afraid of being laughed at. And I won't be, if I can ride Prince. Besides," Nick explained, head down, "after today – I want to do it."

Turtle broke the silence. "What do you think, Dayton?"

"It's worth a try. It may give us something fun to focus on."

"Mack?" Jerry inquired.

The wrangler, slouched in the corner of a sofa, glared at Nick with a blank expression. "He's not gonna win anything," Mack predicted. "But if he's willing to try, I'll help him."

"Let's do it then," Jerry decided. "Mack, why don't you sign up for the events and coach Nick? I'll announce the news at breakfast and make arrangements with Jaremba. I need the rest of you to pump up the campers if this is going to work."

Mack got right to work with Nick – strategizing. "Prince is fastest on the straight-away. So let's skip the Clover Leaf and Pole Bending events. They're too busy and full of twists and turns. Let's stick with simpler events like Speed'n Action and Down-an-Back."

"What are they like?" Nick asked.

"Basically, you race your horse down the course, practically sit him on his butt with a stop-and-turn move, then race back to the finish line."

"I've worked with Prince on some moves like that."

"Good, let's plan on practicing tomorrow."

About noon the following Thursday, two bus loads of campers arrived at the fair grounds. All during lunch, Nick kept an eye out for Jaremba's truck. He wanted Prince to have a chance to relax before the 3:00 PM start time.

When it got to be 1:00 and Prince had still not arrived, Nick walked to the horse barn to size up the competition. At the first box stall inside the door he saw a slender man, his dad's age, in jeans and plaid shirt, cowboy hat pushed back on his head, tooled boot resting on a hay bale, polishing the silver trim on his padded saddle – the Mackinac Island cowboy all over again. If it wasn't him, it might as well have been. A bridle with a long armed, curb bit and braided reins hung next to a brass name plate and a set of blue ribbons. When the horse hung his magnificent, well-groomed head over the half-door, Nick had to admit, maybe Mack was right. Maybe he was out of his league.

A horn honked in the distance, it was Jaremba bouncing over the ruts, waving out the window as he pulled up in his manure spattered truck. Someone was with him.

"Hey, cowboy!" Tanya yelled as she scrambled down from the cab and joined Nick at the tail gate. "Jaremba told me about the horse show, so I asked to come along. I didn't know you would be riding."

"Yeah, I'm going to give it a try," Nick said with less confidence than he had ten minutes earlier. "Nice to see you here," he acknowledged before hopping onto the tire and patting Prince through the open slats. "Come on, guy. Let's get you out of there and onto solid ground." Tanya and Jaremba lowered the ramp while Nick untied Prince. The pinto stopped at the edge of the truck. Looked right. Looked left. Raised his head and whinnied a loud challenge. As he high stepped down the ramp, Tanya said, "So you're going to kick butt with this monster." She shuffled to the side. "He really scares me. Looks like he can whip anyone."

"You got it," Nick replied, amazed at Tanya's knack for saying exactly what he needed to hear.

Nick led Prince to a hitching rail. Tanya, following at a safe distance, acted bored and detached, but her eyes were everywhere. She leaned on the rail next to Nick and thrust her chin toward a group of late model pickups attached to color coordinated horse trailers. "They sure have some fancy wheels over there," she said. "But I bet they aren't air-conditioned like Zaremba's."

Nick reached down to give her five.

"And what are they doing over there?" she laughed as they both watched a horse getting shampooed.

"Can you imagine Jaremba giving his horses a bath?" Nick asked. "Rain water maybe, and that's about it. And I can tell you for sure, you're never gonna see us braiding manes and putting black polish on our horses' hooves."

"Still," Tanya said, "those other horses do look a little more together than our Prince here, all covered with dust and dirt. Tell you what. Why don't I help you hose him down at least? Can't hurt."

They were washing Prince when Nick heard a familiar, heek, heek, heek, behind his back.

"Finazzo's Pet Parlor," Rob mocked in a high-pitched telephone voice holding his thumb by his ear and baby finger by his mouth. "We take care of your split ends, split hooves and tangled mane."

"Who is this guy?" Tanya whispered.

"He's a senior at my high school."

"Poor you," she sympathized.

"Be sure to use conditioner next time," Rob teased. "Can't shampoo without conditioner, you know. Don't want him to become unmanageable."

An hour later, the loudspeaker blared: "Speed'n Action Events begin in 15 minutes."

Feeling apologetic at first, Nick bridled and saddled Prince with the simple, functional camp gear. Prince, on the other hand, seemed not to be intimidated by the expensive tack on other horses. He danced and pranced, snorted and whinnied, as if he thought he could beat anyone. Nick fed off his horse's excitement and tried not to think about his CAMP WA–TONKA T-shirt and baseball cap in the sea of cowboy hats and pearl buttoned Western shirts that swirled around him.

The loud speaker announced, "The first contestant for the Speed 'n Action event is Jim Thompson from Grayson Farms riding Topper's Luck."

A chunky black gelding accelerated past the timing light and thundered toward three small barrels about 50 yards away. He passed the center barrel on the right, checked, turned, passed the center barrel on the left and roared back in front of the cheering grandstand to skid to a halt inside a box drawn on the ground.

"Time: 10.126!"

"Prince," Nick whispered, "I bet we can beat that."

When it was their turn, the time to beat was 9.325.

"Nick Finazzo from Camp Wa-Tonka riding Prince."

Prince shuffled and side stepped. He wanted to run. Tanya and Jaremba waved from the stands. Nick wanted to wave back. No way, he told himself. Be cool like a professional athlete. Concentrate. Put on your game face. Ignore the crowd.

Prince nervously back pedaled toward the side of the arena. Mack leaned on the top rail; his face blank, challenging. 'Let's see if you're as good as you think you are,' he seemed to be saying.

What am I doing here? Nick panicked.

WA-TON-KA! WA-TON-KA!, the campers chanted, faster and faster, building pressure, as if they were shaking a can of soda. This is for them, he thought, as he popped the reins forward. Prince exploded across the course, turned, and roared back. Nick waited for exactly the right moment, braced himself, yanked the reins hard. Prince lowered his weight behind his outstretched legs, slid. One foot was out of the box when he stopped.

"Time: 9.102. Line fault. Disqualified. Nice try son!"

Mack joined Nick outside the arena. "Nice going," he said, patting Nick on the shoulder. "Prince is really faster than I thought," he conceded. "The rest is timing and touch. Let's see how you do in the Down-and-Back."

Nick nodded. Now do you believe me? he felt like saying.

Since there was a half hour break until the next event, Nick treated Tanya to a soda.

"You looked good out there," his neighbor said.

"It's not about looking good," Nick replied. "It's about doing good. You miss by an inch, you might as well miss by a mile."

"Tell that to the campers in the stands. Winning is only part of it. You're their man out there."

How does she know this stuff? he wondered.

"Look over there," Tanya said, pointing to Prince. "Someone's messing with your horse."

Nick recognized the blond hair pulled into a short pony-tail. "That's all right. I know him."

"Sure looks like he loves horses," Tanya observed. "Can't stand them myself. But now, look at him, he's acting like that animal means something special."

Ahead of her for once, Nick interrupted, "Yeah, you got it. Prince was with us when his horse was killed."

Nick watched Bob talking to Prince – saw him talking to Cutter on the first day of camp, in the thicket by the Jordan River, by the side of the highway.

"I bet it's hard for him to just sit and watch," Tanya prompted.

'Timing and touch,' popped into Nick's brain. Mack had just said that. If anyone had timing and touch, it was Petzer.

Nick made a decision. It felt right. He was doing the right thing.

"Bob," he asked, "would you ride Prince for me?"

"Bob Petzer from Camp Wa-Tonka riding Prince!" the announcer called out.

The campers went wild. PET – ZER! PET – ZER! PET – ZER!

Mack, standing next to the arena with Nick and Tanya on either side, explained, "Prince is fast enough. Down-and-Back may be his event. I bet he can break 8.75"

Bob took his time when they called his turn. He sat for a moment patting Prince on the shoulder, staring down the course at the single large barrel. Then he did something no one else had done. He jogged Prince into a gentle canter in a small tight circle, almost like he was winding up a spring. Finally, on the third time around, at the precise moment when they were aimed straight down the course, he lowered the reins and Prince blurred by, heading down, coming back.

But what Nick really saw was the rider. In slow motion. It was his body. The way he moved with the horse. Helping him. Talking to him with his weight, posture and legs.

"Time: 8.669. That's good enough for second place. Nice ride, son! We enjoyed having you boys from Camp Wa-Tonka. Come back next year, all right?"

Mack joined the swarm around Petzer and Prince. Nick and Tanya continued to lean on the rail, relishing the moment. Tanya poked Nick on the shoulder, "That was a nice gift."

Nick smiled.

Outside the arena, Mack cornered Bob. "Listen, there's still time to enter him in the flag race!"

Bob patted Prince, then looked over at Mack, "No, thanks, this was enough. I just wanted to prove that our horses are special – not just camp horses."

Later, Bob helped load Prince onto the truck. Then he squared his shoulders, facing Nick. "Thanks," he said simply. "It's been good knowing
you. I wish I had a brother..." he trailed off.
...like you, Nick finished in his head.

Z
Z
Z
Z
Z
Z
Z

Chapter 15

Wrapping up the summer

Ten days later, work-week was over, campers gone, mattresses stacked, shutters locked. Jaremba had taken his horses for a long winter rest. Tanya had gone back to Flint. Nick had written his name on the ceiling of the bunk house.

Tomorrow he would be going home. He couldn't sleep. Thoughts kept exploding like asteroids in an arcade game. It will really be good to see Mom and Dad and the kids. For about ten minutes. Then I'm going to be bored. Will I be able to horseback ride somewhere around Detroit? Will I come back here next year? When I come back next year, I'm going to get some real boots. Like Mack's. When I come back, I'm going to be able to bug the rookie junior counselor, "Tonight's the night...."

Joe Novara

Joe grew up in Detroit in an Italian neighbor-hood called Cagalupo. Summers up north at a horse camp repre-sented a chance to escape the crowded confines of the motor city's lower east side. Horses have always meant freedom and the rush of fresh air. Joe lived in Italy for a number of years, learning Italian, living with his relatives in Sicily and traveling around Europe. He has spent a summer in Mexico and in Malta, visited Spain, Greece and the Holy Land, and has ridden horses in a rain forest in Puerto Rico, around the pyramids in Egypt, in Tuscon and Taos, Encinita and Queretaro, Tamasopo and Tennesee.

Joe has his Master's Degree in communica-tion from Wayne State University and has taught speech and writing at a number of colleges and universities. Joe lives in Kala-mazoo, Michigan where he continues to work in communication, training and writing.